big & SMALL

Original Korean text by Cecil Kim
Illustrations by Hye-yeong Bae
Korean edition © Yeowon Media Co., Ltd.

This English edition published by Big & Small in 2015
by arrangement with Yeowon Media Co., Ltd.
English text edited by Joy Cowley
English edition © Big & Small 2015

Distributed in the United States and Canada by
Lerner Publishing Group, Inc.
241 First Avenue North
Minneapolis, MN 55401 U.S.A.
www.lernerbooks.com

ISBN: 978-1-925186-06-2

Printed in the United States of America

Rapunzel

A story by the Brothers Grimm
retold by Joy Cowley
Illustrated by Hye-yeong Bae

A poor couple lived near a castle.
In the castle garden were lettuces,
big and green and crisp.
The wife, who was pregnant,
looked at them longingly.
"I am craving for lettuce,"
she told her husband.

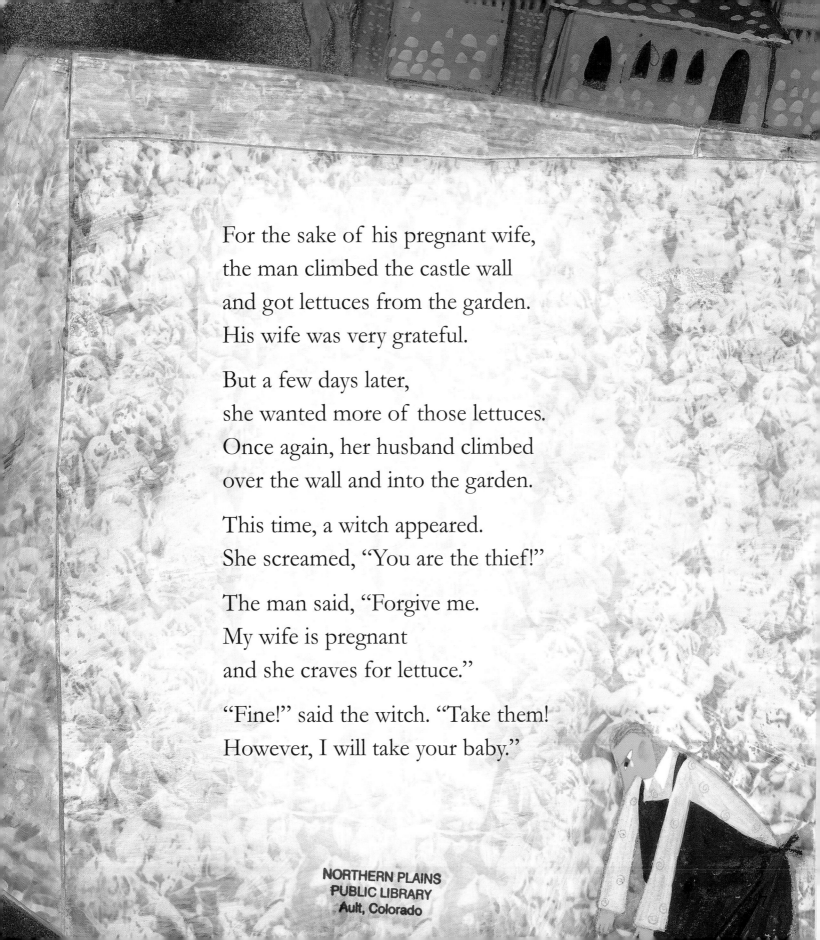

For the sake of his pregnant wife,
the man climbed the castle wall
and got lettuces from the garden.
His wife was very grateful.

But a few days later,
she wanted more of those lettuces.
Once again, her husband climbed
over the wall and into the garden.

This time, a witch appeared.
She screamed, "You are the thief!"

The man said, "Forgive me.
My wife is pregnant
and she craves for lettuce."

"Fine!" said the witch. "Take them!
However, I will take your baby."

When their beautiful daughter was born,
the witch came to the house.

"She is mine," said the witch.
"I will call her Rapunzel.
The name means lettuce."

When Rapunzel was twelve,
the witch locked her in a room
at the top of a tower
that had no steps up to it,
and only one window.

Every day,
the witch came to the tower
with food for the girl.
She called to her,
"Rapunzel, Rapunzel,
let down your hair."

The girl let down her long blonde hair
and the witch would climb to the window.

Many years passed.
A prince passing by,
heard singing in the tower.

Here I am in this tall, tall tower.

If I were a dove, I would fly away.

"What a sad song," said the Prince.
"I wonder who is singing it."
He looked for a way up the tower
but there were no steps.

The prince was so charmed by the song
that he went to the tower every day.
One day, he heard the words of the witch.
"Rapunzel, Rapunzel,
let down your hair."
Golden tresses came tumbling down.
The witch grabbed the hair
and climbed to the top of the tower.

As soon as the witch left,
the prince looked up and shouted,
"Rapunzel, Rapunzel,
let down your hair."
Once again the golden hair came down.
The prince grabbed it and climbed up
to the window of the tower.

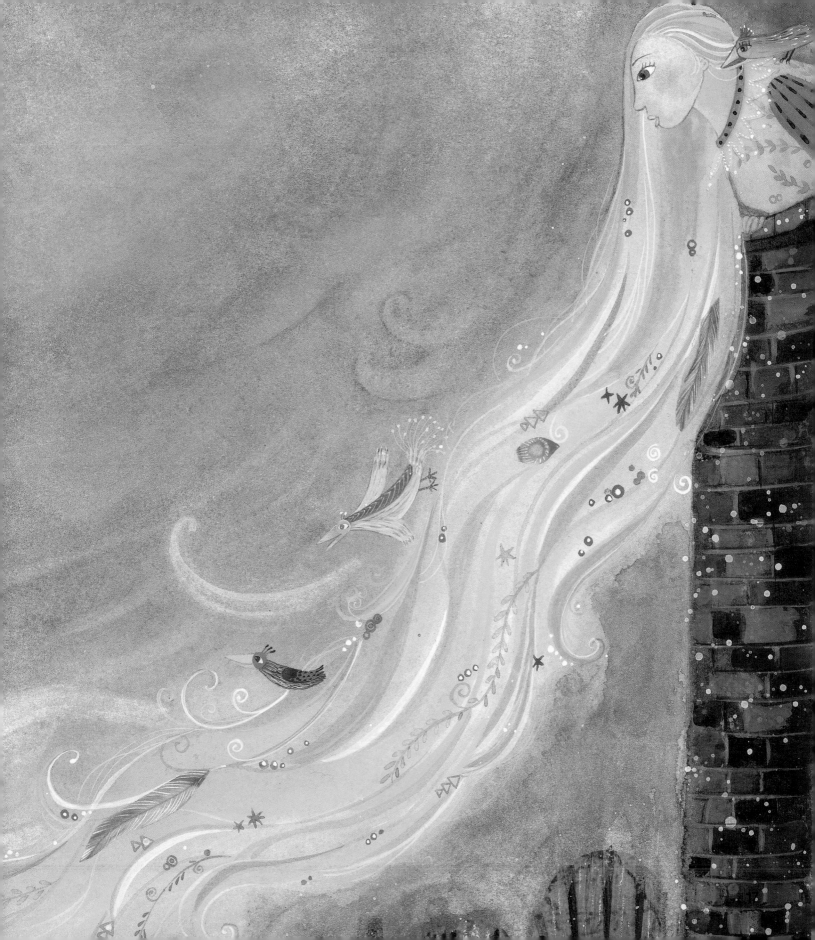

When Rapunzel saw the prince,
she was very surprised.
"Who are you?" she asked.

"I am the prince of this land,
I followed the sound of your voice.
I have loved your sad song
and now I love you.
I want you to be my wife."

Rapunzel said sadly,
"Alas, I cannot get down
from this tower prison.
Bring me bundles of silk
and I will make a rope."

19

Every day the prince brought silk,
but the witch found out about him.
She was furious with Rapunzel.
"You tricked me!" she cried,
and with her sharp scissors
she cut off the girl's hair.
Then she cast a spell
that sent Rapunzel
to a distant place.

That night, the prince called
from the bottom of the tower.
Down came the golden hair,
but holding it at the top
was the wicked witch.
When the prince arrived
at the top, she let it go.

"You'll never meet her again!"
the witch cackled as he fell.

The prince did not die.
He landed in a thorn bush
that broke his fall,
but the thorns pierced his eyes
and he lost his sight.

Blindly he roamed the land,
looking for his Rapunzel.

One day, he heard a song.

Where is my prince?
If I were a dove,
I would fly to him.
I would fly.

27

"Rapunzel! Rapunzel!" he shouted.

"My prince!' she cried and ran to him.

Her teardrops fell onto the prince's eyes,
and a miracle happened.

"Rapunzel! I can see you!"
he cried.

The cured prince took Rapunzel
to his palace, where they were wed.
Their marriage was blessed
with great happiness,
and the witch was never seen again.